Go Away, Dog

STORY BY JOAN L. NODSET
PICTURES BY PAUL MEISEL

HarperTrophy®
A Division of HarperCollinsPublishers

HarperCollins®, 🏠®, Harper Trophy®, and I Can Read Book®
are trademarks of HarperCollins Publishers, Inc.

Library of Congress Cataloging-in-Publication Data

Lexau, Joan M.
  Go away, dog / story by Joan L. Nodset ; pictures by Paul Meisel.
     p.   cm. — (A my first I can read book)
  Summary: An old dog's friendly persistence slowly convinces a young boy
to take him home.
  ISBN 0-06-027502-2. — ISBN 0-06-027503-0 (lib. bdg.)
  ISBN 0-06-444231-4 (pbk.)
  [1. Dogs—Fiction.]   I. Meisel, Paul, ill.   II. Title.   III. Series.
PZ7.L5895Go   1997   96-27272
[E]—dc20   CIP
                                                                      AC

❖
Visit us on the World Wide Web!
http://www.harperchildrens.com

Go away, you bad old dog.
Go away from me.

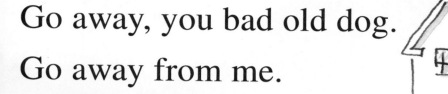

I don't like you, dog.
I don't like dogs at all.

Big dogs, little dogs.

Any dogs at all.

I don't want that stick.

Don't give it to me.

If I throw the stick,
will you go away?

9

There now, go away
with your stick.

11

What do you want now?
If I throw it again,
will you go away?

Don't jump on me, dog.
I don't like that.

Go away, you old dog.
Go on home now.

14

Don't you have a home?
Well, that is too bad.

But you cannot

come home with me.

Don't wag your tail at me.
I don't like dogs.

17

You are not bad for a dog.

But I don't like dogs.

Say, do that again.

Roll over again, dog.

Say, that is not bad.

Can you shake hands?
This is how
to shake hands.

Don't lick my hand.
Stop that, you old dog.

If I play with you,
will you go away?

All right, let's run, dog.

Can you run
as fast as I can?

You can run fast all right.

That was fun, dog.

Maybe we can play again.

But I have to go home now.

No, you cannot come.

Go away now, dog.

Don't look so sad, dog.

Don't lick my hand.
Can I help it
if you don't have a home?

Why don't you go away?
You like me, don't you,
you old dog?

Well, I like you, too.

All right, I give up.

31

Come on home, dog.
Come on, let's run.

21765